Dinosaur School

DINOSAUR BIRTHDAY PARTY

Joyce Jeffries

Please visit our website, www.garethstevens.com. For a free color catalog of all our high-quality books, call toll free 1-800-542-2595 or fax 1-877-542-2596.

Library of Congress Cataloging-in-Publication Data

Jeffries, Joyce.
Dinosaur birthday party / by Joyce Jeffries.
    p. cm. — (Dinosaur school)
Includes index.
ISBN 978-1-4824-0742-6 (pbk.)
ISBN 978-1-4824-0760-0 (6-pack)
ISBN 978-1-4824-0741-9 (library binding)
1. Birthday parties — Juvenile literature. 2. Birthdays — Juvenile literature. 3. Children's parties — Juvenile literature. 4. Dinosaurs — Juvenile literature. I. Jeffries, Joyce. II. Title.
GV1472.7.B5 J44 2015
793.2—d23

First Edition

Published in 2015 by
Gareth Stevens Publishing
111 East 14th Street, Suite 349
New York, NY 10003

Copyright © 2015 Gareth Stevens Publishing

Designer: Andrea Davison-Bartolotta
Editor: Ryan Nagelhout

All illustrations by Contentra Technologies

Printed in the United States of America

CPSIA compliance information: Batch #CS15GS: For further information contact Gareth Stevens, New York, New York at 1-800-542-2595.

DINOSAUR BIRTHDAY PARTY

By Joyce Jeffries

Gareth Stevens
PUBLISHING

Today is my birthday party!

I invite my friends.

Mom hangs a
birthday banner.

Dad blows up balloons.

I get a birthday cake.

Mom puts candles on it.

My friends sing to me.

I make a wish!

I blow out the candles.

My mom cuts the cake.

The cake is yummy!

We have ice cream, too!

We play fun games!

We draw pictures, too!

My friends give me gifts.

I open my gifts.

I got a basketball!

We shoot hoops with it.

I got a bike.

I go for a ride!

Dinosaur Birthday Party